The Tale
of
Black-eye Jax

by

Peter Clover

You do not need to read this page – just get on with the book!

First published in 2009 in Great Britain by
Barrington Stoke Ltd
18 Walker St, Edinburgh, EH3 7LP

www.barringtonstoke.co.uk

ISBN: 978-1-84299-689-8

Printed in Great Britain by Bell & Bain Ltd

AUTHOR AND ILLUSTRATOR ID

Name: Peter Clover

Likes: Sunshine, hugs and Pot Noodles.

Dislikes: Grey rainy days, lumpy porridge and bullies.

3 words that best describe me:
Comical. Crazy. Caring.

A secret not many people know:
I am an alien from the planet Gal'Axor.

For Alan, Trish and Fleur the furry angel.

Contents

Chapter 1
A Bad Start

My name is Harry Moon. I'm nine years old but quite small for my age. I've got a sister. Her name's Charlotte. She's eight and a lot bigger than me. I call her Charlie. She calls me Titch. But that's OK, 'cos she's scared of the dark and I'm not.

I'm really brave so nothing scares me!

So there we were on the first day of our holiday. Mum, Dad, my sister Charlie and me

1

in the car. We had been driving for hours but now, as the car made its way down the steep hill into Robbers Valley, I could see The Highwayman's Inn, set against the muddy river-bank below.

The river was normally a slow, lazy water-way, which bubbled past the inn. Mum had said that. She read it from the guide book when she told us about where we were going! But after all the rain we'd been having over the past week, the river was now flowing so fast that it looked as if it was about to burst its banks.

Bushes and tangled branches had been ripped from the river-bank and pulled into the water. They hurtled past, dragged along by the current. A plastic dustbin lid was blown from the inn's yard onto the rushing water, skimming along like a Frisbee.

Looking out from the safety of the car, I began to worry. When I was telling you how brave I was, I forgot to say that I don't like fast flowing water.

When I was little I once slipped down a river-bank and Dad had to fish me out. The water was fast and black. It came right up over my head. It was only for a few seconds, but it felt like hours. Even now I shudder when I think about it. So with the river like it was, right from the start, I felt that this wasn't going to be your normal, 'no worries' holiday.

We were staying at Robbers Rest – an old cottage with a thatch roof. It was only a mile or so down river from The Highwayman's Inn. Grey sky, pouring rain and massive floods weren't what you'd call a great start to a holiday.

"I hope there's electricity in the cottage, and that all the lights work," said Charlie. Then she stopped worrying about her fear of the dark, by turning to me and adding, "the river seems so angry, doesn't it, Titch. It's so dark and rushing."

Thanks for that, Charlie! I said to myself.

We pulled up outside The Highwayman's Inn to collect the keys to the cottage, and hurried across the cobbled courtyard through the front door.

I pulled up my hoodie to shut out the noise of the river. The water roared so loudly in my ears I thought my head was going to burst. Distant memories came flooding back.

It felt warm and cosy inside the inn. The entrance smelled of lemon furniture polish and old beer. A log fire burned in the enormous brick fireplace. But even with the fire, a shiver somehow managed to run up and down the length of my spine as we entered. All the tiny hairs on the back of my neck suddenly stood on end. It felt as if someone was behind me. Watching me. I felt invisible eyes burning through my hoodie, into the back of my neck. It was really spooky.

I turned around, slowly. Then I gasped. Behind the bar hung a huge, life-like painting of a highwayman. He wore a dark coat and stood with his arms crossed – a pistol held in each fist. He wore a black patch over one eye. His good eye stared right out of the painting, glaring at me. It was Black-eye Jax. The moment I saw him, I felt a cold touch of a hand on my arm.

But nothing scares me, so I just laughed it off. Simple as that.

Dad picked up the keys from the barman.

"Terrible weather," said Dad.

The barman looked totally bored.

"River looks fit to burst," added Mum, shaking a million water droplets from her brolly onto the thick, blue carpet.

"The river did burst once," uttered the barman, suddenly waking up. "Two hundred years ago to this very week it was. The valley flooded when the river ran wild."

Charlie's eyes almost popped out of her head. I felt sick.

Flooded! I said to myself.

"That black mark on the wall over there," pointed the barman enthusiastically, "shows the flood-line, where the water stopped."

"Wow!" gasped Charlie. "That must have been so awesome." She immediately ran over to the water-mark. The flood-line was level with Charlie's eyes. That meant it would have been way over the top of my head! A shudder ran through me. You see – Charlie hates the dark. And I'm really scared of drowning.

"That flood made history," the barman went on. He was really enjoying this, now. Me and Charlie were all ears – we just couldn't help ourselves. The barman pointed to the huge painting behind him with a nod of his head. "Sadly, a young boy drowned. The boy was searching for his dog down on the river-bank." Again, I felt a shiver. "But it was the end for Black-eye Jax," the barman added, "the famous highwayman who used to rob any traveller who dared pass through the valley on their way to the next town, Riverminster."

"Wow!" said Charlie. "He sounds really horrible."

"The Night-Rider they called him," said the barman, "the most feared and dangerous robber alive. Black eye. Black horse. Black heart. He would lie in wait along the river bank. Then, as the horses and carriages slowed down to cross the old stone bridge, he would suddenly appear in front of them like a big, black shadow. He'd block their path on his huge horse, hold pistols to the travellers' heads, and rob them of their money and jewels."

"What happened to him when the river flooded?" asked Charlie.

"He drowned," replied the barman.

"How?" I asked.

"No one really knows for sure," said the barman. "But I've asked around a lot, because I'm writing a book about him. And local legend says his body was found, one morning, washed up on the river-bank – dead – with a look on his face like a frightened rat."

Chapter 2
Something's Coming

It didn't take us long to settle into the cottage. Within five minutes, all the bags were unpacked and their contents stashed into cupboards and drawers.

Dad wasted no time, and soon had a roaring fire burning in the living room. It wasn't as good as the fire at the inn, but it looked and felt homely.

Charlie was smiling a lot now. She'd checked out all the lights and made sure they were all working. The dark, gloomy cottage was flooded with light.

Outside, the river roared past the front door. I couldn't get away from it. Everything else was fine. It was just the river that was spoiling things a bit for me.

I stood with Charlie, outside on the porch. The rushing water swirled and rolled past us like a muddy brown roller-coaster. It threw spray up at the windows. And rising waves slapped the river-banks with horrible gulping sounds – just like someone gasping for air.

"What if the water comes into the cottage?" said Charlie.

I wish she wouldn't come out with things like that, I thought.

"Well, it might mess with the lights," I teased back, giving a nervous laugh.

OK! So I didn't mind much about the cottage suddenly being in darkness. Candles could be cool. But the thought of the cottage filling up with murky water from the river scared the pants off me. And nothing is supposed to scare me!

"Come on in, you two," yelled Mum. "And keep away from that river-bank."

I didn't need to be told twice.

It was getting darker. A huge orange sun-ball was sinking slowly, like a giant peach, behind a dark line of trees.

The rain was now only a drizzle as me and Charlie took one last look at the bubbling waterway. It seemed to be roaring even louder in our ears. And then we heard a completely different sound. Far away, behind the trees, beyond the light of the setting sun. Somewhere in the darkness beyond the river – we both heard something strange. Something really weird.

"What's that?" asked Charlie. "Is it the wind?"

I remember shaking my head. It wasn't the wind. It sounded more like a horn – a hunting horn, or something like that. I'd heard one in a film once on TV. The horn sounded its hollow call along the stretch of water-way, right to the front door of our cottage. It seemed to be coming up-river from The Highwayman's Inn. It was so weird. It made me shiver. My skin goose-bumped.

Then we heard the distant thunder of pounding horse's hooves. Fast hooves, moving at a gallop. Nearer ... closer. The air around us suddenly turned freezing cold. Our breaths made small puffs of mist, as the horn

sounded again, and a black rider came racing into view, thundering along the river-bank towards us.

In the semi-darkness, both horse and rider had a strange, shimmering glow to their dark outlines. The horse was huge!

We both stared. Charlie grabbed my arm. It was just like a nightmare. Then we gasped as a terrible chill gripped our stomachs, filling us both with a fear much greater than darkness or the bubbling river. We suddenly saw the rider clearly for the first time, bent low across the neck of his demon stallion.

"I ... I can see right through him," gulped Charlie. "I'm sure I can."

"Me too." My voice suddenly sounded very faint and scared.

We both stared hard as the ghostly rider pounded swiftly towards us. He was cloaked in a long, dark coat and wore a three-cornered hat with a long black feather, stabbed in at the side. The hat hid most of his face. I think that's what scared us the most. Not being able to see what he looked like. Until he lifted his head.

We wanted to run. But our legs had turned to jelly. A terrible white face, wearing a black eye patch, was grinning at us through the grey drizzle. His one good eye glared at us with an evil glint.

"Black-eye Jax!" I mumbled. "It's the highwayman."

Charlie opened her mouth to scream, but nothing came out, only air.

Suddenly our legs could move again. We ran inside and slammed the door shut. But Black-eye Jax had already vanished, back into the dark, moonlit night.

Chapter 3
A Walk Into Danger

That night I dreamed I was in a storm and was trying to crawl along the trunk of a fallen tree. The tree lay across a river like a bridge. I was trying to grab a small, cold hand – reaching out to me through the bubbling water. It was a nightmare of deep, dark, rushing water.

The dream was so real. I remember trying to wake myself up. I tried really hard, but the dream was strong – it held me fast.

Below, in the roaring river, was a boy. He looked a bit like me. He was holding onto a tangled mass of branches that were trailing in the water. The foaming river bubbled over his head, dragging him down.

"Help me!" His thin cry was lost on the wind as the fierce current pulled him away from my grasp.

I opened my mouth to call out but my voice was a whisper. I had failed. Everything was still and silent.

Then, through the dream, came the sound of a hunting horn – sounding through my head. I don't remember anything after that. I woke with my heart beating fast. But when I told Charlie the next morning at the breakfast table, she said, "That is just soooo weird, Titch. I had that very same dream last night."

We just looked at each other in shock. We were close – brother and sister close – but this kind of thing had never happened to us before.

Outside, nothing had changed. The rain was still teeming down.

"It's raining, it's pouring. It's mouldy and boring." Charlie pressed her nose against the window pane and made up songs while I finished off six bits of toast and jam.

"Don't worry," said Mum. "It won't come into the house."

"What?" I said.

"The river," smiled Mum.

"But it came into the Highwayman's Inn, didn't it?" Charlie reminded us. "Right up to here." Her hand shot to a level way over her head. Then she looked at me and gave a shrug. "Sorry, Titch."

She just can't help herself, can she? I thought.

"I don't suppose this seems like much of a holiday for you two, so far, does it?" said Mum.

Me and Charlie both had to agree. It wasn't quite Centreparcs.

"We thought we'd take a trip out today! Ride the local bus into town," Mum said. "Do a bit of shopping. Rent a DVD player and get some films for you both to watch."

That sounded better.

The local bus was an old single-decker with big shiny bumpers and huge head-lamps. It stopped on the top road just above the cottage, then it went back past The

Highwayman's Inn and made its way slowly through Robbers Valley into Riverminster.

"Can we get some cartoons?" asked Charlie, peering out at the rain through the bus window. "And if they've got *Finding Nemo* can I get that, too? It's the best DVD of all time."

Mum smiled. "Of course you can, Charlie. And cheer up, it can't rain forever," she added.

"We can stop off at The Inn on the way back if you like," said Dad. "And have a spot of lunch in their snack bar."

"There's a children's playroom – like a small arcade at the back," said Mum. "'The Hideout,' I think they call it." Me and Charlie perked up at that idea. We looked at each other. We both instantly thought of Black-eye Jax, but we didn't say any more about our strange dream. We were too busy thinking about what films we'd get.

The town of Riverminster was wet and grey. We found a few boring shops and at last, one that rented DVD players and films to holidaymakers like us. I got *Spiderman*, a pirate film and *Shrek III*. Charlie chose a selection of her favourite cartoons which she'd seen a trillion times before. And found a copy of her beloved *Finding Nemo*. Then we came back.

Like Dad suggested, we stopped off at The Highwayman's Inn for a snack. Charlie and I had the same – sausages in batter with chips. We mixed mustard and ketchup together and invented '*tomusto*'. Mum and Dad had shepherds pie with millions of green peas. The pies were huge. They must have had a whole shepherd in each one.

Afterwards, Mum and Dad read magazines and all the newspapers while me and Charlie looked for the Hideout.

We had to pass the main bar to get to the games room. We both tried not to look at the massive painting of Black-eye Jax, hanging on the wall behind the bar, as we ran past.

"Don't look at it," hissed Charlie. "Just look straight ahead."

"But I can feel him staring at me," I said. It was just as if a ghostly hand was reaching out from the painting to grab us. We broke into a run and tumbled down the steps into the small arcade.

The Hideout wasn't that bad. There was this brilliant racing car game – Monster Wheelies – and I got to level three, no probs. Charlie spent all her time staring at a glass cabinet stuffed full of pink teddy bears. She lost all her money in seconds trying to grab one by the ears with the metal arm of a wonky crane!

"You two seem to be enjoying yourselves," said Dad when he finally came to fetch us.

"Level three," I boasted.

Charlie stuck out her bottom lip and sulked.

"I really, really wanted one of those teddies," she said. "I was just getting the hang of it."

"Tell you what," smiled Dad. "I've just had an idea. It's only one stop down the road to the cottage. Why don't you both stay here a while longer? The next bus is in one hour. It stops at the top road, right above our cottage." Dad smiled and gave us both a two pound coin, plus bus fare home. "I'll go back there now, with Mum, and set up the DVD. You two stay for another hour and have fun."

"Brilliant," grinned Charlie.

"Level four and pink teddies," winked Dad as he turned to leave.

That hour passed really quickly. But to be honest we didn't spend all of that time in the arcade. And we didn't catch that bus home, either. I couldn't get past level three and Charlie kept dropping her teddies. We spent our money in ten minutes flat.

"If we could just have one more go," moaned Charlie, "we might get lucky."

"But we can't," I reminded her. "We've got no more money left."

"What about the bus fare," she grinned. "Dad left us extra for the bus. We could use that. Like Dad said, it's only one stop. That's not far. We could walk it, Titch, no problem. Just follow the river-side path."

"Mum and Dad would go nuts."

"They'd never know," said Charlie. "If we left in five minutes, we'd get there way before the bus, anyway."

Charlie had a point! I had to admit it.

"We could wait at the bus stop, on the top road above the cottage," she added. "Then, when the bus comes along, we pretend we've just got off it!"

It was a great idea.

"It's a master plan," said Charlie. "So let's do it, Titch. Unless, of course," she added, "you're chicken. Scared of walking along that little old river."

"Nothing scares me," I said. So we did it.

Chapter 4
Hooves of Thunder

We had spent the bus fare home – but level three stayed well out of my reach. And Charlie was only able to rip a leg off a sad looking teddy when the grabber got stuck and went crazy.

"Better than nothing," I joked. Charlie threw the teddy's leg at my head.

"Suppose we'd better get going, then," she moaned.

"Well it was *your* idea," I reminded her.

Outside, it had started drizzling again. I pulled up my hoodie. Charlie flicked on her cap. We sneaked out of the inn by the back door and set off on the river-side path down to the cottage. After five minutes Charlie started huffing. "It feels like we've walked at least 50 miles."

Typical, I thought. *She had started to complain already.*

Charlie pulled her cap down further over her ears.

"We could phone Mum," she said. "Look, there's a phone box by that picnic area over there. If we had the money to make the call, Mum would come and get us in the car."

I told Charlie to shut up and keep walking.

It was getting a bit dark now. Black clouds had suddenly slid across the sky.

Charlie gripped my arm.

"What's up?" I asked.

"Listen! I thought I heard something." The tall trees along the river path had now become thick, dark shapes against the darkening sky. Leaves rustled in the sudden breeze that chilled the river. We both began to shiver. The rain stopped, but it had turned cold. A strange mist began to curl up from the river. We put our heads down and walked faster. We didn't like this at all. Suddenly this seemed a very bad idea.

Three minutes later, we could see the cottage, up ahead of us. Then we heard that same chilling sound. Someone was blowing a hunting horn. The haunting call made us both stop in our tracks.

Our mouths hung open as we looked at each other in horror. The horn sounded again! It seemed to be calling to us. We both turned slowly, to look back. Then we gasped together, almost in the same breath, as a black rider on horse-back stormed out of the river mist and galloped towards us.

My heart was thumping so hard in my chest it hurt.

"Black-eye Jax," gulped Charlie. And she was dead right. My heart then skipped a beat as the word "*dead*" kept repeating itself madly inside my head – like a DVD stuck on play-back.

Thundering hooves were almost upon us. We'd never felt so scared in our lives. The horse was huge and as black as night. Black-eye Jax glared down at us with his one good eye. His mouth was set in a cruel grin. I thought I heard him laugh.

We both started to run. My legs felt all wobbly but the cottage was just up ahead. Charlie was away like a rocket. I was amazed at how fast she could move. My hoodie slipped and I could feel the horse's cold breath on the back of my neck.

My legs seemed to have lost control. It felt like I was running through thick mud.

Then Charlie fell. I caught up with her and pulled her quickly to her feet. We ran again. The sound of the hooves was even louder than the roar of the river. The hunting horn screamed again. And Black-eye Jax was upon us.

Cold fingers reached out and grabbed my hoodie. Then a strong hand pulled me up into the air. My legs kicked out as they left the ground. Next thing, I was flung across the horse's back with Black-eye Jax sitting right behind me. A horrible smell of damp earth

and rotten leaves stung my nostrils. I tried holding my breath but I was soon gasping for air, too terrified to look anywhere but straight ahead.

Then it was Charlie's turn. Her mouth opened in a scream as the Highwayman grabbed her, but Charlie made no noise. Suddenly, everything went silent. Black-eye Jax pulled Charlie up across the saddle to join me. We clung together for dear life. We trembled with fear. It was awful.

Then we heard his voice. Only two words were spoken. "You're needed," he whispered, close to our ears. The Highwayman's voice was thick and gruff. Suddenly we both felt freezing cold. Our skin was like ice.

Without warning, the horse suddenly took a flying jump, crossing the river in one massive leap. *Thump*. We hit the ground on the far bank, then thundered back along the river, away from the cottage!

"Please," yelled Charlie. "Please, take us back. I want my mum."

"You're needed," whispered the Highwayman. "I can't reach him."

We didn't know what he meant. Well, not at first. But he kept repeating those words, over and over again. "You're needed. I can't reach him."

In the end it was Charlie of all people who said, "I think he needs our help, Titch."

There in front of us, we saw the boy in the river. And we both understood.

It was just like the barman's story, when the river burst its banks. It seemed that history was somehow repeating itself – 200 years later.

Chapter 5
River Rescue

A boy was in the river, clutching madly at the bank with his arms out-stretched. His faint cries for help were lost against the roaring rush of water.

"Hold on," I yelled. "We're coming."

It was dark. As black as night-time. A huge moon had suddenly come out, and the river seemed ready to burst its banks. Time was moving fast. Too fast.

Thunder boomed somewhere far away. And above us, a flash of lightning turned the river-bank a ghostly white.

Black-eye Jax let us down.

"Hold on," I called to the boy again.

"I can't," the boy gasped as a great rush of water burst over his head. He suddenly lost his grip and Charlie cried out as the current took him away, swirling his body down-river, back towards the cottage.

We watched with our mouths hanging open as he bobbed up, gasping for air. Then somehow, he grabbed hold of the branch of a fallen tree. The tree had lost its hold on the bank when the river had eaten away the earth from its roots. Now it leaned out low across the water. Almost like a bridge – from bank to bank. Just like in our dream!

We ran to the fallen tree. I stood, staring at the trunk, stretching across the rushing water. A chill of terror gripped at my stomach. The river looked so angry. I couldn't move.

"I'll hang on to your legs, Titch," called Charlie. "Or if you like, you hold mine and I'll crawl out and try to reach him."

No way could I let Charlie do that. I looked back up the bank. Black-eye Jax was standing there, a tall black figure against the pale moon. He raised the hunting horn to his lips and blew. That sound will stay with me forever. My skin tingled. The hairs on my neck stood on end. But suddenly I felt much braver. The fear of water was all around me. But somehow, I knew I could beat it. The fear was strong – but so was I.

"I can't hold on much longer," cried the boy.

In an instant I lay flat on my stomach and began to shuffle along the wet, slippery bark. I clamped my legs around the smooth trunk and slowly made my way forward.

"Go on, Titch," Charlie urged me on. "You can do it."

The water gushed and roared below me, dark and dangerously close. If I slipped! … the thought of it made me shudder. I wished that Black-eye Jax could help. Why couldn't he? Why couldn't he just fish the boy out of the river, himself? Then I got really scared. What if he knew I was going to die? What if he'd brought me and Charlie here to drown in the dark, black river, just like he had drowned, 200 years ago? Maybe Black-eye Jax had tried to save the boy! Was that why he couldn't help – because this was where his life ended. Or maybe he was scared of the river – like me. My mind was spinning.

"Hurry," called the boy. "Please hurry." But suddenly I couldn't do a thing. My arms and legs had stopped working and I was shaking all over. I felt myself slipping. And a huge spray of water suddenly gushed over my back.

Then I heard Charlie scream.

That was it. That was when I lost my hold and began to slide, head first, into the cold, black water. I wanted so much to wake up. This had to be the worst nightmare ever!

But someone was there, in a flash, grabbing my ankles. The hands were ice cold. They were small, yet strong. And very determined. My head came up out of the water. I looked back. I couldn't believe it. It was Charlie.

"I've got you, Titch."

I don't know how she did it, but Charlie somehow managed to pull me back up onto that tree trunk. My teeth were chattering. Charlie's hands were frozen.

"Hang on a bit longer, Charlie," I said, stretching down and out as far as I could, towards the black water.

"Reach up," I yelled to the boy.

"I can't," he cried. His eyes looked terrified.

"You must." I tried to flatten myself against the trunk and reach out even further. But the tree was very wet and slippery. I didn't like this at all. I was so scared.

"Just a bit further, Titch."

This time I grabbed the boy's hand and pulled him closer.

"Climb up over me," I said.

The boy was tired but he dragged himself up out of the water and began to crawl over my back. Gasping for air, we both struggled forwards along the trunk. Charlie followed up behind, and we were soon all standing safely back on our side of the bank, close to the river-path walk.

Then something terrible happened. There was a great creaking noise and the tearing, ripping sound of wood splintering. The river had lost the boy and now, in anger, it wanted another vicitm. We looked on in horror as the tree was torn clean out of the bank and went hurtling down-river, crashing first against one bank, and then the other – its branches smashed and broken.

I looked around. Suddenly the air felt different. Clearer. Lighter. The moon wasn't there anymore. The dark sky had lifted. And Black-eye Jax had gone.

Chapter 6
A Boy Called Jax

The boy's name turned out to be Jax –
which was quite amazing!

"Where do you live?" asked Charlie.

Poor Jax looked worn out. He was shaking
like a leaf, and shivering with the cold. He
looked around. He seemed really confused.

"Up there," Jax said. He pointed to a
worker's cottage up on the top road. "We

only moved in a few weeks ago. My dad's got a job down at the inn while he's writing his book. Dad's nuts about the legend of some Highwayman who used to live around here. Dad's sure that we're related, somehow in the past. He even named me after him."

Just then, we heard the final call of the Highwayman's hunting horn, somewhere far away.

Charlie and Me just stood there with our mouths hanging open.

"What are you two staring at?" asked Jax, shivering. "I came down here looking for my dog. I thought he might have fallen in the river." Jax's voice trembled as he spoke. "Then I got a bit too close," he said, "and slipped down the muddy bank."

At that moment, a small, black dog came barking and bounding towards us, through the trees.

"Barney!" cried Jax, falling to his knees. The little dog jumped up, licking Jax's wet face.

"There's something stuck in his collar," noticed Charlie.

Jax pulled out a long, black feather.

"He must have gone running off after a bird," said Jax.

What kind of bird has feathers like that? I thought.

Charlie and Me looked at each other. That feather was just like the one stabbed into the side of Black-eye Jax's hat!

"You won't tell my dad, will you?" said Jax, suddenly worried. "He'll go mad if he knew I was down here. He told me always to keep well away from the river."

"And we're supposed to be on the bus home," I said. "So don't you say anything, either."

"Where are you staying?" asked Jack.

"Robbers Rest," we told him. "It's just a bit further down river."

We realised that we could still see the cottage. It wasn't very far away. Suddenly, the bus came flying along up on the top road, above us.

"Come on, Titch. Move it," yelled Charlie, grabbing my arm. "If we leg it, we can still make it back in time."

Leaving Jax standing alone and looking a little puzzled, we ran the 200 or so metres along the river path. This had turned out to be a real adventure holiday.

Out of breath and almost bursting, we stumbled up to the front of the cottage. It felt great, beating the bus. But not so great when I turned to Charlie and said, "How are we going to explain our clothes being soaking wet?"

Charlie gave a shrug, just as Mum opened the front door and threw a bowl of water and potato peelings all over us!

Charlie screamed.

Mum looked horrified.

"I am so sorry," she said. "I can't believe I just did that," she tried to explain. "I just heard the bus go by on the top road, but I never thought you'd get down here so quickly."

I looked at Charlie and we both burst out laughing. Then Mum started to laugh as well, but she still kept on saying sorry, which was great. We'd actually got away with it.

"I am so sorry, guys," said Mum. "I was just throwing out the peelings – I thought the ducks by the river might like them. You'd best get those wet clothes off and change. Dad's set up the DVD and all your films are waiting."

"Shall we watch *Finding Nemo* first?" giggled Charlie as we squelched inside, dripping wet. "We just love being under the water, don't we, Titch!"

Mum shot me a worried look. But it was OK. Charlie was so right!

"Great choice," I said, following her upstairs. I gave Mum a wink. Somehow I knew that I would never be scared of water again!

Barrington Stoke would like to thank all its readers for commenting on the manuscript before publication and in particular:

A. Lacey

Ross Lacey

Julia Littler

Simon Littler

Benjamin Petch

Catherine Petch

Become a Consultant!

Would you like to give us feedback on our titles before they are published? Contact us at the email address below – we'd love to hear from you!

info@barringtonstoke.co.uk
www.barringtonstoke.co.uk